REDEEMING THE MOUNTAIN MAN

IRIS WEST

To you, my reader. I hope you love Blossom Ford, and the sexy men, curvy women and kind but extremely interfering folk that live there, as much as I do.

CHAPTER ONE

Isabella

SWEAT DRIPS DOWN my back, and my forehead is clammy. I wipe it with my forearm as my eyes scope the dirt path in front of me, looking for signs of the cabin I know is near. I've only been walking ten minutes, but already, the altitude and rough terrain is getting to me. If summer hadn't come early to Arizona and my sneakers weren't digging into my feet, I'd be enjoying the fresh air and beauty of the mountain.

Instead, I'm wondering how the hell a person lives in a place that is so hard to get to. I suppose Pararescue Jumper Riordan O'Connor is not like most regular folk. He can probably trek up this path a hundred times without breaking a sweat. For over twenty years, he was away at several war and disaster zones and rarely came home. He's been back for about a year, but is rarely seen in town.

His brothers wouldn't have any trouble either; there isn't a single ounce of fat on their sexy bodies. But what about his parents? Or girlfriends? I shake my head. My thoughts shouldn't be going there.

I square my shoulders and keep stepping forward, ignoring the pinch on my feet. Clem's trusting face spurs me on, the girl's smile infectious, despite her long battle with leukemia. Her dream is to be a para-rescue jumper, like Riordan, who's a national and local hero. Her wish is to meet him and I desperately want to make that wish come true, as a professional and as someone who cares about Clem.

The wooden cabin appears suddenly. One moment, all I can see are trees and shrubs, but then, a beautiful log cabin stands before me, like an oasis in the desert.

It takes a while before I figure out where the door is. I stumble on it just as I'm about to give up the search and call out a greeting. It looks like the rest of the walls of the house and doesn't have a handle. I so badly want to take my feet out of my sneakers and massage them, but I know how much first impressions count.

I plaster a smile on my face and knock. It wears out when a couple of minutes go by without an answer. I knock again and wait, my eyes shifting to the truck in the yard. Surely Riordan wouldn't go far without it.

The door opens as suddenly as the cabin showed up. There's no sound. Alarm wipes away my smile, but only for a moment. My lips lift again, as I look up and up until I meet a pair of deep-set gray-blue eyes.

They are more striking in person than they were in the newspaper. Not just his eyes. My head probably only reaches the top of his broad chest. It's hard to know for sure when I'm trapped in his arresting gaze.

"Can I help you?" His voice is cold, curt, yet something in it fascinates me.

I blink. Remember to smile.

"I'm Isabella Thomas, from the Blossom Ford Wish Foundation. I'm here because one of our little girls, who's very ill, would love to meet you, Mr. O'Connor. She's a huge fan of yours. You're her hero."

Arms cross and I spot the tattoos that run up his forearms and disappear into a t-shirt stretched tightly across a solid chest of bunching muscles. The ink is so vivid; I want to reach up and trace the patterns on those thick arms. They are so intricate, it must have taken forever to do them.

"I answered your letter with a no."

He pushes the door toward me. I shove my foot in the narrowing gap and close my eyes, expecting pain to shoot up the limb the moment the door bangs on it. A couple of beats later, I open them. The door is a breath away from my foot.

"May I use the toilet, please? I won't make it down the mountain."

I hate to use this card, but there's no other choice. Most people, especially those from Blossom Ford, would let me in. Riordan looks at me with an impassive face.

"Please." I'm no longer pretending. I was fine before, but using the word toilet has made me want the damn toilet. There's no way I will survive the walk to my car and drive down to town; I'll either wet myself or be in agony.

He gives me a once over. I don't know if it's because of the genuine desperation on my face, but he opens the door wider and moves back.

I dash in, afraid he'll change his mind.

"Second door on the right," he says in that crisp voice of his, but it's too late. Now I know he has a conscience.

When I return to the sitting room, Riordan is standing there like he's waiting to usher me out.

"May I have a glass of water? I'm parched."

I wish I knew him better so I can interpret his signature distant look. I follow him out of the living room.

He moves gracefully for such a big man. I like the way he strides confidently, hands in his pockets, muscles bunching under his shirt and low-slung jeans.

When he opens the refrigerator, I see his face again. For the first time, I notice the silver in his mustache and beard. I hide my hands behind my back to stop the itch to pet it. I've always found older handsome, but Riordan O'Connor is making me wish we are two people that are meeting in a bar somewhere.

He's way older than the few men I've dated, though.

And there's no knowing if he's at all attracted to me, like I am to him.

He fills a glass with cold water and places it on the kitchen table. I set my bag beside the glass and sit down.

"It was a bit of a struggle to come up the last few yards. I suppose everyone says that when they visit you."

He grunts.

I drink slowly, thinking about how I can get him to open up. Little Clem is such a darling, and she's counting on me.

He opens a cupboard, removes a first aid kit and gets out a band aid Slowly, he puts it on the table and slides it to me.

"If I'm not mistaken, you have a blister. Put it on."

I blink up at him.

He makes a sound of impatience, then gets down on his knee and turns my chair so it's facing him. His movements are measured the whole time. He removes my right sneaker and sock, turns my foot clockwise and anticlockwise.

I'm surprised by how gentle his fingers are. What else would he be gentle with? I tell myself to get my mind out of the gutter. Riordan is used to treating people. There's probably nothing in his mind apart from making sure I'll get down the mountain safely. Perhaps he wants to ensure he doesn't have to rescue me.

He places the band aid on my heel, the brush of his

thick fingers on my skin sending pulses of electricity along my nerve endings.

I shiver.

His eyes fly to mine and my breath stutters. The cold ice has been replaced with fire. Stormy, gray-blue eyes glide over my heated face and linger on my lips. I wait, hoping, hoping for something, because in that instant, I know Riordan O'Connor is a passionate man capable of giving a woman a good time in bed.

CHAPTER TWO

Riordan

I'VE BEEN CELIBATE all my life and although there have been women I wanted to fuck, I've never felt the searing attraction that strangled my cock at the combined sight of Isabella Thomas' curvy body in tight jeans; a top that hugs her bounteous breasts like a glove and the innocent smile on her face.

While I'm the opposite, she embodies sunshine and hope. She's like a siren promising a mix of decadent pleasure and sweetness, and I like that she came up here and didn't give up, even when her foot was obviously hurting. She must have been hot too, if the drops of sweat on her forehead were any sign.

The need to kiss her full, cherry lips is driving me

crazy. I never lose track of what I'm doing when I'm working on a patient. And right now, that's what the woman sitting in front of me, looking like a queen ready to be loved, is.

I know I'm being a dick. She deserves to be treated with honesty, decency. A better man would flirt with her and show her a good time.

Thinking about another's look on her body causes a wave of ice to splash through my body. I mentally shake my head. I have no right to feel jealous or want Isabella Thomas.

"You're good to go." I release her foot.

She blinks, confusion in her gaze.

Fuck it, I did that.

I stand and lean against the counter, away from her intoxicating cherry scent and soft brown skin, hands in my pockets.

She clears her throat. "About Clem, I really hope you'll reconsider. I don't know if you had the time to read-"

"I read it."

"She drew something for you." Isabella places a paper on the table. "She knows you may have a lot on your plate, so she asked me to say it's okay if you can't meet her. She's just glad a national hero who won a Medal of Honor lives in the same town as her and can call you her idol."

My hands fist. I know she caught the movement when her eyes shift to my jean pockets.

"But I hope you'll meet her, just for a few minutes. She may not have long to live and this would make her day."

"I heard you."

I take the paper she slides across the table and study it. It's a drawing of a man pulling along a woman and a child from what looks like bomb induced debris. The kid's handwriting is terrible, but she has a way with drawings. The para-rescue jumper motto, tattooed on my back, is drawn across the top of the image.

"These Things We Do, That Others May Live," Isabella says the motto quietly.

Even her voice is pleasant to hear, which is surprising because usually, nothing is better than silence.

"There are many ways to save someone, Mr. O'Connor. You're like a miracle to Clem. If you can meet her, it'll be like there's hope that the miracle of a suitable donor showing up and a transplant might come true."

Hope can keep a person going. I saw that in battle fields and disaster areas. But I'm no longer the type of man that knows how to make a girl laugh. I haven't done that in over twenty-seven years. I can give her nightmares, but not hope. Unless she's waiting to be rescued from a war or disaster zone.

I'm about to return the picture when I catch the hope in Isabella's large brown-black eyes. It cuts at me.

I don't give a fuck about what others think about me, yet I don't want to see the brightness in that sweet gaze dim.

I want to be someone who only gives her pleasure, makes her laugh. Which is a joke, considering I know even less about making women happy.

"I'll think about it."

Her face lights up further. There's no other way to describe it. A dimple forms on each of her cheeks and her even white teeth flash.

Something in me moves.

Mine

I want to make her feel that happy every day. I certainly want to be the only man that makes her anticipate a kiss the way she did earlier, when I applied a band aid to her heel.

How can I be the man for her, though? I learned to kill before she was born. I might be good at saving strangers' lives, but I wasn't any good when it came to making sure those I love stay safe. Isabella would be better off with a much younger man, one who'd fit right in with her young lifestyle and could chat to her just as much as she loved talking.

CHAPTER THREE

Isabella

IT'S PIE CONTEST Day, and I'm at the town square setting up a tent for Miss Georgina, a regular donor to the Aid Foundation. It's eleven in the morning, but it's boiling already, the sun scorching its way across the large green.

I always loved Pie Contest Day when I was little. Some kids at the orphanage hated it. In a way, so did I. It was hard seeing our friends with their moms and dads when ours weren't part of our lives anymore.

For me, it was a chance to dream about the kind of family I'd like to have. And the treats. In return for helping, we'd get sweets, cake and pie. I'd keep mine in a piggy jar, Mrs. Gallagher–the orphanage director - gifted me and eat one a day until the next time I could stash away more candy. The more I helped, the more treats I received.

I'm struggling with a pole when Lorcan, Riordan's younger brother, passes by my tent, hands full of decorations.

"Someone is coming to help, Sweetheart, I promise," he hollers as he dashes past.

"That's what you said ten minutes ago, handsome. Get yourself together," I holler at his back.

It would be so much easier if Lorcan was the O'Connor I had the hots for, instead of his grumpier brother. He's handsomer and easy going. But something about Riordan calls to me; I can't stop thinking about him. On second thought, Lorcan is a no go too. He isn't interested in anything serious.

"Hi, Bella. I brought help,"

I glance up at Lorcan's Mom, say hello and thank her, trying to see behind her for whoever the unfortunate person might be, from my sitting position. It's almost impossible to resist Mrs. Shauna O'Connor when she asks for a favor.

A couple of seconds pass, then Riordan steps in front of the stall. Hastily, I stand up.

"I'm not sure you've met my eldest, Riordan. If you need anything, he'll give you a hand."

She beams at me then throws her son a loaded glance before heading back toward her own tent.

Riordan is as handsome as he was two days ago when I dropped by his place. Like the other day, his face is unwelcoming. There's little doubt he was blackmailed into helping. He looks like he wants to be anywhere but here.

"I guess it's just as hard for you and your brothers to say no to your mom as it is for non-family members."

He grunts.

He marches to the opposite side of me and picks up a pole. I mirror him, expecting him to take over, like some guys do.

By the time the tent is half up, I have a different type of respect for Riordan, other than that of a citizen to a soldier who keeps her country safe. Instead of bossing me around, he worked with me, respecting what I'd already done on my own. He speaks only when he has to, every word seemingly carefully chosen for maximum efficiency.

"How are you finding retirement?" I ask, because I'm dying to learn more about him and now I know what I'm doing and don't need to concentrate, it's hard to resist my curiosity.

"Okay."

His eyes are on the tent, but he answered. I tell him about how hard it was to adjust to Blossom Ford after being away in a large city for college, even though I'm glad to be back to the only place that's home.

I want to know why he's so quiet. Did his experiences in the military turn him into a taciturn man, or was he always like this? He's not on any social media. All I could find about him is what's in the papers. He's a very well-respected soldier, nationally and locally.

Miss Georgina returns, lugging a bag. Riordan takes it from her.

"Where would you like it, Miss Georgina?" He asks.

"Over there." She points to one corner of the tent we've almost finished putting up.

It takes up a couple more minutes to finish setting up.

"We'll get a couple of tables," Riordan says.

We carry tables back and help the pensioner set up her stall.

"Thank you so much, you two. I'll be okay now. Can you help Penny set up? Her granddaughter is running late."

A couple of hours later, we've helped set up a few more stalls and the afternoon festivities are about to start.

"Would you like to grab a drink?" I ask Riordan.

"I'm good. About Clem, if she's expecting a friendly guy with jokes up his sleeve, she might be disappointed. I'm a soldier of few words."

"All she wants to do is shake your hand and say thank you. She may have a ton of questions about joining the para-rescue jumpers, though."

"When is the best time for her?"

Was he worried about what to say to Clem? Is that why he initially refused to meet?

I'm starting to like Riordan O'Connor. He's helpful and kind and is not afraid of hard work. But, I can't tell if he returns my feelings.

He was careful to keep his fingers from touching mine. Apart from that blazing look of lust in his cabin, there's nothing that suggests he's attracted to me, let alone likes me.

CHAPTER FOUR

Riordan

CLEM'S STARING OUT the window when we walk into the kids' ward, late afternoon the next day. I've seen enough sick people to know if Clem doesn't get a transplant soon, she'll have a very hard time surviving.

A few kids wave to Isabella and she waves back, her expression one of pleasure. She enjoys working with these kids, loves making them happy.

"Clem, guess who I have here," Isabella says softly.

Clem turns away from the window and glances at Isabella, then at me. Her hand flies to her mouth. She stares at me like she didn't believe I was going to come, even though Isabella mentioned the twelve-year-old was looking forward to my visit.

I feel Isabella close the curtain around the bed but keep my eyes on the girl.

"Mr. O'Connor?" her voice is a squeak.

I introduce myself formally and shake her hand. Her hair is black, but otherwise, she looks so much like my sister Fiona. The same hopeful green eyes, the same slender frame, though Clem is two years older than Fiona was when she passed.

Her eyes shift over my full uniform and medal.

"You can sit on the bed," Isabella says.

Clem wants to know about some places I rescued people. I keep the gruesome stuff to myself and reveal only what I can, but her eyes light up when I describe a couple of missions I was in. We also spend a few minutes going over her drawings.

"What's the likelihood of her finding a donor?" I ask Isabella once we're in her office.

"She's been waiting a while and is high on the list. We're all keeping our fingers crossed for her."

I march to the window and watch patients, staff members and the general public go about their business on the street three floors below, as I process the helplessness I feel inside. There are so many jackasses in the world. If anyone must die, why can't it be one of them? I've lived a full forty-four years. Why not me and not a brave girl like Clem?

"It's hard to understand, isn't it? I'm always wishing I could do more than I'm already doing."

I face Isabella. She's such a cheerful person. How could someone like her cope with facing the sadness she must witness while doing her job?

"Isn't it hard? Dealing with shit like this?"

The ghost of something painful flickers across her eyes. "It is, very much so." She inhales. "I'm the only survivor of a car crash. My parents and brother didn't make it. I was five."

My heart aches when I think about how lost the little girl she was must have felt. Platitudes didn't work for me, so I keep silent. Listening is the best I can do for her.

My memories are faint, but I recall our family cherishing life. I want to give back to society for being alive and I also want to enjoy everything I can for my family's sake. I just feel that's the best way to remember them, to live my life to the fullest.

I swallow. We're so different. What happened to Fiona was my fault. Isabella had no fault in what happened to her family. Yet, her words wash away some of the darkness in me. I want some of the sweetness and warmth that's such a fundamental part of her.

Slowly, her hand snakes out and touches my beard. I watch her, aware this could be dangerous and tell myself it's an innocent touch, a person comforting another. I repeat that to myself, as I lean toward her, also wanting to offer comfort.

I swear that's the truth. At least it is until our mouths touch. Then it's all about the fire. Her lips are hot and welcoming beneath mine.

The small sound she makes when I slip my tongue

inside her mouth has me crushing her to my hard body.

"Siren," I say softly, enjoying the way her arms wrap around my neck.

"Hmm?" she murmurs into my mouth.

I kiss her again and again, like a man drowning.

The rake of her hands down my back drives me wild.

My hands slide down her back to her curvy ass and I squeeze the flesh there, pulling her even closer.

"Siren, you taste so fucking good."

I kiss down the side of her neck and double back to nibble her earlobes. She whimpers and I feel like I did well.

Laughter sounds outside her door. My arms tighten around Isabella.

She's shaking. Worried, I tip her head up. Mirth fills her eyes and curves her lips.

"I'm done for the day. Do you want to go to my place?" She asks.

Her body is warm against mine. I'm powerless to resist the playful look in her eyes and am nodding before I've formed a conscious decision.

CHAPTER FIVE

Isabella

MY TINY LIVING room feels smaller with Riordan in it. Even when it's girls' night and my sisters of the heart are here, it doesn't feel as small as it does now.

Something is off. Riordan seems nervous. I'm not sure how I know that, but I'm suddenly sure of it.

He's studying the pictures on my wall, hands fisted in his pockets. Maybe it's those fisted hands that make me think he's nervous. Or it's me. The only time I've felt this nervous around a man was when I was a virgin.

I grab two beers, close the short distance between us and hand him his.

"Thanks," he says. "Is that you?" He points to the largest frame on the wall.

"With my parents and brother."

"You were cute."

"Not anymore?" I can't resist teasing him.

His lips twitch.

I drink the icy cold yellow liquid, a smile hovering around my lips.

"Still cute," he says distinctly.

"So are you." The words slip out.

His eyes narrow. "I've been called many things, this the first time I'm hearing that."

It was the way he was standing before, in front of my family. The nervousness about him. But I can't tell him that, not yet.

"I suppose you're used to hearing words like sexy and God's gift to women."

His cheeks turn pink. Is he blushing? He walks away from me.

"I've been around men too much for that kind of talk. Who are the women in this picture?"

"Part of my found family. Aiyana, the woman with the huge sombrero, grew up in the orphanage with me. I met Carmen and Briana at school." I tell Riordan how the four of us became friends as we sip our drinks.

When his lips twitch again at the part where Aiyana gave Mary Beth a snail as a sign of friendship-causing mayhem, I decide I want to see him smile and laugh often.

He moves around my sitting room, examining the paintings on the walls.

"You have an eclectic collection of paintings. You

must get a lot of these. Who does this belong to?"

"A little boy that was born with three kidneys. Isn't he a genius with a pencil?"

Riordan squints at the picture as if trying to find a meaning behind the array of colors. "It helps brighten up your place. It may also have a deep meaning I can't fathom."

I laugh. This time, I'm sure he's joking.

His lips lift only a fraction, but it feels like we've crossed a bridge.

"This is Clem's work," he says.

"How did you guess?"

"Does she ever draw anything other than para-rescue jumpers?"

"Now that you mention it, no. I never noticed it." I play with the condensation on the beer bottle. "What do you do to unwind?"

Riordan finishes the last of his beer. His Adam's apple bobs up and down.

I'm so in lust with this man.

It's surprising I'm drawn to someone so opposite to me. Everyone I've dated has been just as gregarious as I am.

"Mountain climbing, fishing and nature watching."

They are so like him. "I used to nature watch a lot when I was younger. I still do it every now and then. It's one of Aiyana's favorite things to do. Another beer?"

"Better not. I'm driving."

You could sleep over.

I'm proud of myself for not blurting that out.

I sit on the sofa. Riordan joins me.

"You're beautiful, Siren. I want to be inside you so badly, I hurt."

I like his pet name for me. I like the way he says it even more. It makes me feel special.

"I feel the same way. I've been thinking about you since the day I met you at the cabin."

He traces his finger across my bottom lip. I open my mouth and slide my lips down it, sucking on it like a sweet.

"Jesus, Siren."

The roughness in his voice turns me on, but Riordan suddenly stands up. Rakes his fingers through his black curls.

"What's the matter?" I can feel the tension in him.

"I want more than one night." His gray eyes are tortured, like he's warring with himself.

"So do I, Riordan. Let's date."

"I'm twenty years older than you, Isabella."

"So what? I can do math, too. I like you. Each time we spend time together, I fall a little more for you. There's nothing wrong with that."

"You should be with someone who's full of cheer, like you."

"Cut the bullshit and be honest with me, will you?"

Riordan's eyes skate over the flat before finally resting on me. "I'm so sorry, Isabella."

He marches away without a backward glance.

CHAPTER SIX

Riordan

I'VE CLIMBED THIS mountain every day since I left Isabella on Monday. It's Friday afternoon, so it's quiet up here. Just the way I like it.

It's taken me a few hours to reach the top. If I slipped, the likelihood I'd survive is slim, so even though I climbed a lot of mountains during my career, I focused every part of my brain on what I was doing.

The absolute focus stopped me from thinking about Isabella for a few hours, but as soon as I reach the top, she's the first thing on my mind.

Being up here is breath-taking and humbling. Everything feels small and inconsequential. Isabella's words seem truer.

I can't shake the feeling that I've been running away from my pain for twenty-seven years. Me, who ran into danger for just as many years. Yet, it seems I'm a coward when it comes to my emotions.

I inhale the clean mountain air then descend the mountain, glad again to give up my concentration to surviving.

The sun is setting when I reach the cabin. A curse slips out when I spot Isabella marching in the yard.

"What are you doing here? Do you know how dangerous it is to traipse around the mountain at night?"

She places her arms on her hips. "Why do you care?"

"God damn it, Isabella." I glare at her. She could seriously hurt herself.

She glares back, brown-black eyes almost black.

I've never seen a woman look more beautiful. I've fallen so hard for her, I can't even think straight around her.

At least she's wearing appropriate footwear.

"What the fuck is the matter with you, Riordan? You want me as much as I want you. It's fine if you don't want to date me. If you can't tell me why, that's fine too. But don't walk away from me, as if I don't even deserve an answer. I thought I meant more than that to you."

"You do."

I hate the way I made her feel unsure of herself.

"Then, talk to me."

"Come in."

I shower quickly, my body aware of Isabella's

presence, only a few feet away. When I enter the living room, she's sitting cross-legged on the floor, checking out my record collection. It's one of the few things I kept from my life before the army.

I want to see her sitting like this every day.

I sit and watch her quietly until she turns around and spots me. She doesn't even look startled that I've been here for a while. I like that; it means she's getting used to my ways.

I don't know how to start. For the first time since I was seventeen, I want to talk to someone about the incident that irrevocably changed the course of my life.

I like this side of Isabella too. There's no doubt she loves a good chat, but she knows how to listen, how to wait. The duality of her nature is probably one thing that makes her brilliant at her job. Especially when she's dealing with adult patients.

"I don't know how to date. I've never been in a relationship, not since high school, and that doesn't really count."

Isabella bites her bottom lip. "Do you mean you've only had casual relationships?"

"Like most seventeen-year-old boys, I was a little crazy about girls. I had a steady girlfriend and was in love for the first time in my life. One day, an emergency came up and Mom asked me to watch my siblings. I was listening to something my girlfriend said and didn't see my sister run into the road to save a dog. The bloody dog survived, but not Fiona."

She gazes at me with anguish in her eyes.

I stand and march up and down the space in front of the sofa. "Everyone told me it wasn't my fault, but I couldn't shake the guilt. Everything reminded me of her. She was such a brave little girl, like Clem, only a couple of years younger."

Isabella hugs her knees.

"I left town and joined the para-rescue jumpers. It was only right I should pay back by doing the most dangerous job in the military. I told myself I didn't deserve to enjoy the company of women. Saving lives became my life."

I shove my hands in my pockets and fist them. Isabella walks towards me. She puts grabs my wrists, pulls my hands out of my pockets and tucks them around her back. Then she stretches up and embraces me.

"Do you still feel like it's your fault?"

"Yes. If I'd been watching her, that wouldn't have happened. But I've lived long enough to know it's impossible to control everything because we're only humans."

"I'm glad. Would you tell a mom who lost a child because she was momentarily distracted by a beautiful sight to live the rest of her life paying for what she did?"

"No."

"You've done your penance, Rio. Now, you owe it to Fiona to make the most of your life. That's what she'd want for you. If she was anything like Clem, she'd be kicking your butt right now for not enjoying all the beautiful things in life."

"Would she now?"

"Hmm."

It isn't the first time I'm hearing this, but now, I'm ready to listen. I feel lighter, like I've taken a heavy load off my shoulders.

I breathe in the cherry scent of her hair. It feels natural to pick her up and sit with her on my lap.

"What kind of beautiful things?"

"Dating me, for starters."

She feels so right in my arms.

"It's day one for us," I say, looking into her eyes.

CHAPTER SEVEN

Isabella

RIORDAN PULLS ME down and kisses me. It's a long, sweet caress that leaves me feeling like he won't run away anymore.

When his hands run up the sides of my chest, I sigh in relief, because I am ready for more. I lean back a little, giving him room to touch my front. We both groan when he slides his hands over my breasts, squeezing them.

"I want to touch every part of you."

He stands up and heads into what I hope is the bedroom. I kiss the veins along the side of his neck until a strawberry forms on his tanned skin.

He bites my lip.

As soon as he puts me down, I take my clothes off. Riordan is faster and helps me remove my boots when my jeans get stuck there.

"I love your tattoos." I caress the big one on his chest and watch as it comes alive when he inhales sharply.

I gaze up and find him watching me, eyes ablaze with desire.

He splays his hands on my shoulders and snakes them down my breasts. Reverently, he circles both mounds and squeezes, thumbs rubbing experimentally over my hardened nipples. Then he laps at them, all the while squeezing my breasts until I moan and grab onto him.

"You like this," he says, a boyish smile on his face.

He picks me up and lays me on the bed. His enormous cock is straining against his abdomen. I glide my hand down the length of him, but he hisses and moves away from my touch.

"What's wrong?"

He tucks me against his shaking side.

"Riordan?"

His free hand is hiding his face. I move it away. He's blushing. And he's laughing at himself. "It's so good, I almost came in your hand. I need a minute, otherwise, it'll be all over."

"Is this your first time?" I run my hand along his mustache.

"Disappointed?"

"Nah, I have the feeling you're a fast learner. Just surprised."

"I went past first base a few times, but I wanted the

first time to be with someone special."

"The girlfriend? What happened to her?"

"Jealous?"

"She was special to you."

"She's happily married with kids."

He turns me onto my back and starts playing with my nipples again. "I love you, Isabella. And I fucking love your curvy body. Your tits fit perfectly into my hands."

Shocks of electricity dart through me. Riordan kisses his way down my round tummy and runs his fingers through the black curls on my mound. Then he touches my happy button, rubbing the swollen organ gently, the way I like it.

"Tell me what you like, Siren. I want to pleasure you."

"Just like that. Don't stop."

Steadily, his thick fingers massage me until my hands wring the bedsheets and my hips are gyrating to the increasing pleasure. Riordan inserts a finger into me, then another.

My entire world is centered on his hand and the pleasure he's creating.

"More?"

"Yes."

He takes my clit into his mouth and pulls hard on it.

I cry his name out and come apart, my body shaking uncontrollably. He laps at my juices and causes a round of pleasure aftershocks.

When he blankets my body, I wrap my arms around him, his weight making me feel grounded.

"Open your eyes, Isabella. I want you looking at me when I take you."

He kisses me, and I taste myself. His cock probs at my entrance.

A dart of pleasure pain shoots down my earlobe. My eyes fly open.

"What did I say?"

I touch his cheek with one hand and place my other hand on his cock, guiding him inside me.

"I see you, Riordan."

"You're my first and last, Siren."

He thrusts into me until he's buried to the hilt.

"Fuck it." He inhales and exhales roughly. "You feel so good. I wanted you to remember this first time, but I don't think I'll last long. It feels like your pussy is strangling my cock."

I contract my pelvic muscles.

Riordan groans into my neck.

"Minx," he says after a couple of beats of further breathing.

He kisses me deeply and thrusts into me, slowly at first, then faster, his thick penis filling me fully. I wrap my thighs around his ass and run my hands through his hair.

He slips a hand between us and strokes my clit.

"Come for me, Siren," he growls against my neck.

His seed spills into me and I orgasm in a rush of exquisite pleasure.

"You are mine, Isabella."

I never want to be with anyone else.

"I love you, Riordan. You're mine too."

EPILOGUE

Riordan

Six Months Later

IT'S OUR SIXTH wedding anniversary, yet I never tire of gazing at Angel's soft honeyed face on my chest when I wake up. We got used to sleeping this way. Even on the occasional days I'm held up at the hospital and find her sleeping, we always end up this way when morning comes.

I'm not working today, and the twins are off school. They are trying to be quiet but are making such a racket; I wonder how Angel can sleep through it. She's still refusing to have help around the house and insists on driving the kids to their various clubs. Sometimes her mom, Granny and dad go with her. Although I walk our cocker spaniels Dolly and Rufus before work, they still take up a lot of her time. She insists on coming when I walk them after work. I suppose it's no wonder she's tired.

Three knocks sound on the door. It's Liv. She's so full of energy, she always goes overboard with everything she does.

Liv marches in, followed by the dogs, who are wagging their tails.

"Wow! Seriously?"

She turns away, and I laugh at the fake haughtiness on her shoulders.

"What is it?" Angel wakes and sits up just as the dogs bounce on the bed.

"Mom, I can't believe how you and Dad are still so lovey-dovey with each other. Ew!" She approaches the bed and lays a waterproof tablecloth on top of the cover. "Happy wedding anniversary," she sings to the accompaniments of the dogs' barking.

Ollie walks in wearing an overall, a large tray in his hands. He deposits it gently on the tablecloth and uncovers the plates.

"Happy anniversary, Mom and Dad," he says more quietly.

"This is lovely, sweethearts! It smells incredible too. Did you make the toast, Liv? It's browned just right," Angel says.

"See." Liv turns to Ollie. "Even Mom said so. It's perfect."

I stop myself from laughing at Ollie's raised eyebrow. I catch Angel's eye and know she's attempting the same thing. Our boy is so serious, that even though our doctor says he's growing well, I worry sometimes.

"What do you think, Dad?" Liv asks.

I look at Ollie. He shrugs. "It looks okay to me," I say, smiling at him.

Liv can't cook, no matter how much Angel teaches her. She has too much going in her brain to have the patience cooking requires. Her mind is full of information about stars, comics and the latest exploits into space.

Last year, when he was only nine, Ollie won the Blossom Ford Pumpkin Pie Contest. He was smart enough to do well at school if he applied himself, but his grades were average. He was happiest in Food Technology class. Not only had he memorized all the recipes his teacher and mom taught him; his cooking was to die for.

Liv and Ollie make themselves comfortable on the bed and we tuck into breakfast. It's become one of our traditions. Breakfast in bed on our wedding anniversary. This year was the first I didn't help the kids.

"Granny Jess sent a card," Olly states.

Angel was right about Mom. She'd wanted to spend more time together, but wasn't sure how. We'd never be as close as Angel's family. I feel closer to Angel's mom and dad, still we talk over the phone and see each other more. Dad is still gallivanting about the world, and I wish him well.

Every year, the kids spend a week of their summer break with Lucy's parents, so their biological mom is still a part of their lives. After we confessed our love for each other, Angel put a picture of the twins and Lucy in the sitting room, saying their mom would always be a part of our family.

"Happy anniversary, Hun," Angel says, her sea-green eyes sparkling.

"Happy anniversary, my angel."

I'm looking forward to spending the day alone with my very own angel when the kids go to their grandparents.

The End

MARRYING THE PROTECTIVE PROFESSOR

CURVY BRIDES OF BLOSSOM FORD #1

August

ALL MY LIFE I've secretly wished I was born and raised in an ordinary family, with loving, welcoming parents instead of being the town's sign of bad luck, growing up at Blossom Ford Orphanage and having the town's name as my surname, like the other kids there. I can't help believing if I was wanted, the acceptance and sense of belonging would have helped me become someone who knows how to love. That belief is strongest when I think of Ella Mitchell.

It's Friday night so ensuring she gets home safely is my top priority as I park my SUV a short distance from Jackson's Diner where she's working, far enough to see the door of the restaurant but not so close that anyone might link my presence to the diner. I don't care how the interfering residents of Blossom Ford view me, but I don't want rumors to spread about Ella.

I slide down the car seat, getting comfortable even as I curse myself for the warmth that spreads through my chest at the mere thought of her name. As I've done a millionth time, I tell myself I'm here to protect her.

An uncomfortable tightness in my chest and a bitter taste in my mouth that I'm all too familiar with have me exhaling slowly. But it's hard to chase away the guilt. I cannot keep from committing the same sin. I'm a scarred, divorced, grizzly mountain of a man that's old enough to be her father while she's a beautiful, innocent twenty-two-year-old with her whole life ahead of her. Ella deserves better than me. But I still can't stop thinking about her.

It makes no difference that what I feel for her is more than physical attraction. I love her strength, soft smile and the way she's warm to everyone that crosses paths with her. There's a certainty in my bones that she's meant for me alone. This only makes the guilt worse. I should let her go because I love her.

And I have. To a point. For the last two years since I returned to Blossom Ford, saw her for the first time and fell for the kindness in her honey hued eyes and the sweetest curves I'd ever seen, I've stopped myself from approaching her. From claiming her. At least in real life. Because in my dreams, I've made love to her every single night and spent my days laughing with her. I've always considered my self-control one of my strongest attributes, but I can't stop dreaming about her.

I can't help the fact that I won't have her driving home by herself at midnight, after her shifts at the diner on Fridays and Saturdays. If I'm an asshole, so be it. And if deep down I know as well as ensuring she's safe, I have to see her face, I'll take the guilt and deal with it.

I frown when only two cars remain in the parking lot. One is old Jackson's beat up truck, and the other belongs to Rosie; the woman who works with Ella. Ella's old yellow mini should be right besides Rosie's.

The door to the diner flies open and Rosie marches out in her apron, phone glued to her ear. She sprints to her car. My frown thickens. How is Ella going to get home? Will she be closing on her own? I force myself to stay in the car. As much as I want to rush in and help, keeping a distance is crucial to my self-discipline.

I ramp up the air conditioning in the car a little higher. It usually takes one hour to close, but tonight, it'll take Ella longer. Old Jackson doesn't think hard work hurts women. There's no way he's going to help with setting the dinner to the way he likes it.

I keep my eyes on the door and an hour and a half later, I'm rewarded with the sight of Ella's curvy hips wrapped in hugging denim and the soft way her breasts hug her blouse. Even after a ten-hour shift, she's a vision that gets my heart racing.

She zeroes in on my car and it's like she can see me, like she knows I'm waiting here for her. She does this on Fridays and Saturdays; the days I wait for her. If she worked any other nights, I'd wait for her then, too. She's friends with Mrs. Gallagher, the orphanage director who's the closest thing to a mother I've ever had. Ella must think of me as a much older brother who's looking out for her.

She steps on the street and heads towards me. I know that she's just taking the road to her house, but I can't stop my heart from beating even faster. It's like this every time I see her.

I'm feeling something else too; anger. Her walking alone down the empty street at this time of the night is pissing me off.

She's only a few feet from me when a car careens down the street and stops beside her. I sit up straight, hoping a friend is coming to pick her up. But she doesn't slow down, even after spotting the car.

I scowl as a man stumbles out of the car and steps in her path. It's Toby Anderson, Ella's ex. Something ugly rears in me. Despite my unstoppable feelings for Ella, whenever I see him, I realize how great my self-control is. Every time I saw him with Ella, I wanted to knock him out. The four months they dated were an exercise in self-discipline I didn't think I was going to win. But for Ella, to give her the chance at happiness she deserved with someone her age that could give her a comfortable life, I held myself back.

I don't like the way Toby sways on his feet. The light from the full moon and lamppost in front of the diner are enough to make out the disgust on Ella's face.

Before I know it, my hand is on the door handle, but my eyes don't stray from Toby.

They are talking but the loud music and shouts from the car stop me from hearing what they are saying. Toby reaches out a hand and touches Ella's arm. She wrenches it back.

I'm out of the car. I sprint towards them, her safety the only thought in my mind. for her, I'd tried staying away, but her safety is something I'll not compromise on. even if it means she might hate me for interfering with her life.

MATCHED TO PATRICK

THE O'CONNORS OF BLOSSOM FORD #1

Patrick

MINGLED LAUGHTER DRIFTS from the sitting room, bringing mixed feelings of joy and sadness. We decorated the entire house in green–it's St Patrick's Day. As usual, we've been to church and are now having beef pot roast, which Mom and Aunt Shauna insist on making every year on the feast day of St. Patrick. Dad would have been so happy to hear that laughter. Even though we gathered like today at Christmas, St Patrick's Day was his favorite holiday.

I remove more salad from the refrigerator.

"Ready for the parade of women our moms no doubt have lined up for you this year?" My cousin Lorcan asks. I know his lilting voice like I know my own.

I snap the refrigerator closed. "Will I be the only one

on display?"

He winces. "You're the eldest. And you're Aunt Caitlin's only son, so you'll definitely be in the firing line. Mom will surely want to marry Riordan off first. I'll be an afterthought."

The lump in my throat prevents me from chuckling. I can't really blame Lorcan. I used to be like him. The thought of marriage drove me barmy. Not anymore.

At first I couldn't imagine myself being happy with a family, not with the crushing guilt I felt over what happened to Little Fiona. Before Dad passed, he made me promise to let go of that guilt and cherish the time I've been blessed with. Although I believed it'd never happen, little by little, I'm appreciating life.

I want what Mom and Dad had, though. They were meant for each other. Someone out there is my soulmate and the moment I find her, I'm not letting go. For the last couple of years, Mom and Aunt Shauna's matchmaking efforts haven't bothered me in the least.

I glance outside to where Riordan, my cousin and Lorcan's eldest brother, sits in the spring sun. "Riordan is not ready to get married. I doubt he'll hang around for the picnic and anyone our moms might want to set him up with."

That giant of a man is still blaming himself for what happened to his little sister Fiona, even though it's been twenty-six years since she was taken from us. Our dads were first cousins -both O'Connors. The two of us are forty-four, but I'm older than Riordan by one week. As the oldest children in the O'Connor family, it was our responsibility to make sure Fiona was safe.

Lorcan opens the back door.

"Mom is calling," he says to Rio.

It's the only thing that'll move my eldest cousin. Aunt Shauna may not be calling him now, but Riordan knows she'll soon be, wanting to make sure he spends as much time with us as possible before he scoots up the mountain.

Riordan and Lorcan's six brothers and Dad are watching TV while Mom and Aunt Shauna are chat.

"Don't forget to take good care of my friend Nara when she gets here. She was very kind to me the other day in town when I forgot my wallet," Mom reminds me.

We spend another couple of hours leisurely drinking and chatting, then get up to prepare for the outdoor picnic, which starts at four. The whole town is invited to our farm. Our parents started the tradition a few years after settling in Blossom Ford and starting a lettuce farm together, because they missed spending St Patrick's Day with their large family back in Ireland.

We put up tents on the large grass area between my house and Riordan's. Mom and Aunt Shauna used to do all the food when they were younger, but now, Lorcan gets caterers in to bring sandwiches and other finger food. By the time the townsfolk arrive, Cormac and Emmet, my youngest cousins, have set up a DJ stand which is playing upbeat music and the entire field is filled with green bunting and balloons.

I'm taking a breather from greeting people when I see a woman strolling towards Mom. Something about the way she walks catches my attention. She's wearing black skinny jeans that mold her curvy ass to perfection and a light green top that covers a pair of generous breasts and complements the sun-kissed tone of her skin. Wavy jet-black hair falls below her shoulders and shimmers in the sun.

I'm too far away to see the color of her eyes. Before I know it, I'm marching towards Mom, curiosity and something I can't name, compelling me forward.

"I'm so glad you came, Nara," Mom is saying when I reach her side on a strategic part of the field where she, Aunt Shauna, and their friend Ms. Penny can see everyone.

Tawny, that's the color of her eyes.

I answer myself as Nara greets everyone with an amiable smile that reaches her almond-shaped, yellow-brown eyes and warms the inside of my chest. She's comfortable around Mom, Aunt Shauna and their friends, even though she must be in her mid-twenties. The silver hoops on the tops of her ears glint in the sunshine.

"This is my son, Patrick." Mom points to me.

I stretch out my hand in greeting and when she holds mine; hers is small and smooth against my large and calloused one. I don't let go and she glances up at me.

That's when I know. That I've found the woman I've spent the last few years searching for.

The friendly warmth on her face is replaced by something else: interest. A tinge of pink fills her cheeks before she pulls her hand away.

Her voice cracks a little when she says hello leaving me to wonder where the confidence she exhibited a few moments ago went.

"I'll show you where the food is," I say.

"I don't want to trouble you." She looks about her. "I'll find it, thank you."

"It's no trouble at all," Mom beams at Nara. "Patrick will walk you over to the food area. Just ask him if there's anything you need to know."

A frown forms on my face as I lead the way. At my age, I'm old enough to know when a woman has the hots for me. I know Nara fancies me, but she's decided not to pursue it.

If there's one thing I'm good at, is getting to the root of a problem. Now I've found Nara, I'll have to convince her I'm the only man for her.

OTHER BOOKS BY THE AUTHOR

CURVY BRIDES OF BLOSSOM FORD SERIES

MARRYING THE PROTECTIVE PROFESSOR

MARRYING THE GRUMPY DIRECTOR

MARRYING THE POSSESSIVE NEIGHBOR

MARRYING THE WIDOWED DOCTOR

MARRYING THE SCARRED SOLDIER

MARRYING THE OBSESSIVE CEO

MARRYING THE BIG MOUNTAIN MAN

THE O'CONNORS OF BLOSSOM FORD SERIES

MATCHED TO PATRICK

REDEEMING THE MOUNTAIN MAN

ABOUT THE AUTHOR

Iris West writes short and spicy romance about alpha heroes and the women they can't help falling in love with. She loves reading all types of romance books that have a happy ending and is an avid Kdrama fan.

Follow or like her on Facebook and Goodreads.

FREE BOOK

Would you like a free book? Sign up to my mailing list at https://dl.bookfunnel.com/t191w45ryj to receive a copy of Loving My Fake Husband, a free to subscribers only, Curvy Brides of Blossom Ford Series short story.

HELP OTHERS FIND THIS BOOK

Thank you for reading Redeeming The Mountain Man. If you enjoyed this book, please help others discover it by leaving a review at your favorite online book store.

Many thanks,

Iris xx